Dan's mum is called Isobel and
Nicky likes her a lot.

One very hot day Isobel took
the boys to the seaside.

The seaside town was packed with
visitors.
"Where's the sea?" asked Nicky.
"It must be down one of these roads,"
said Dan.

"But WHICH one?"
"Round and round the roundabout,
past the flowers and trees,"
sang Isobel.

"Round and round the roundabout,
where's the road we need?"
joined in Dan.
"Oh look! There's the right road,"
laughed Nicky.
"It's pointing to the sea."

"It's the one on the corner
by the statue on the green,"
sang Isobel.

At last they found the sea.
"YIPPEE!" yelled the boys.

"Hey! Wait for me," called Isobel.

The boys built a sandcastle and the sea
trickled into their moat.
"I'll keep this shell for my mum,"
said Nicky.

"Listen!" whispered Isobel.
"You can hear the waves crashing on the
sea-shore."
"Oh, come on!" yelled Dan.
"I can SEE them!"

They all ran into the sea, splashing and laughing, then chased each other along the beach.

"Can't catch me!" shouted Isobel.
"Phew! My mum's as fast as the wind!"
gasped Dan.

After their picnic Isobel lay in the sun
and the boys drew pictures on the sand.

"I wish we could stay here for ever and ever," said Dan.

But the day came to an end.
"Time to go," called Isobel.
"Bother!" cried Dan.
"It's getting late," said Isobel.

"Just a bit longer, please," said Nicky. "Come on," she laughed. "If you're really quick we can all have an ice-cream before the bus goes."

They bought their ice-creams then couldn't
remember the way back to the bus.
"Ah, here's the statue," said Isobel.
Then Nicky remembered the song.
"Round and round the roundabout
past the statue on the green," he sang.

"Round and round the roundabout
past the pointer to the sea,"
joined in Dan.

"Now this is the right road,
The one we really need.
It's the road by the roundabout
with all the flowers and trees,"
remembered Isobel.

The bus was nearly full, but people made room for them on the back seat.

They got home late and Nicky gave Mum
his shell.
"Oh, that's pretty," she said and held it to
her ear. "I can hear the waves crashing on
the sea-shore."

"Yes," said Nicky.
"We had a lovely day!"